DATE DUE

MAY 1 7 200	OCT 2 4 200	MAR 2 1 2018	
	DEC 2 3 200		
SEP 0 4 200	APR 0 1 200	DEC 0 6 2018	
OCT	SEP 3 0 200	APR 1 6 2019	
JAN 0	OCT 28 200	OCT 0 8 2019	
	SEP 2 8 2010	OCT 1 7 2019	
OCT 0 6 200	JUL 2 4 2012	MAR 1 9 2020	
FEB 0 7 200	SEP 0		
MAR 1 7 200	APR 0		
APR 0 3 200	OCT 1 5 2014		
	DEC 3 0 2014		
MAY 2 0 2	JUL 2 1 2015		
FEB 0 7 200	NOV 2 5 2015		
MAY 3 0 200	JUL 0 8 2017		

11.96

Discard

BAD THE GOOD MANNERS BOOK

THE BAD GOOD MANNERS BOOK

Babette Cole

DIAL BOOKS FOR YOUNG READERS
New York

Don't leave the water running in the bathroom.

Don't clog the sink up
with hair.

Don't stuff the toilet with paper.

Don't leave your toys

on the stairs!

Don't mess around in the kitchen.

Don't dress the dog . . .

or the cat!

Don't shampoo

with a
big tube
of glue,

and don't tell your mom

that
she's fat.

Do try

to dress
yourself

correctly.

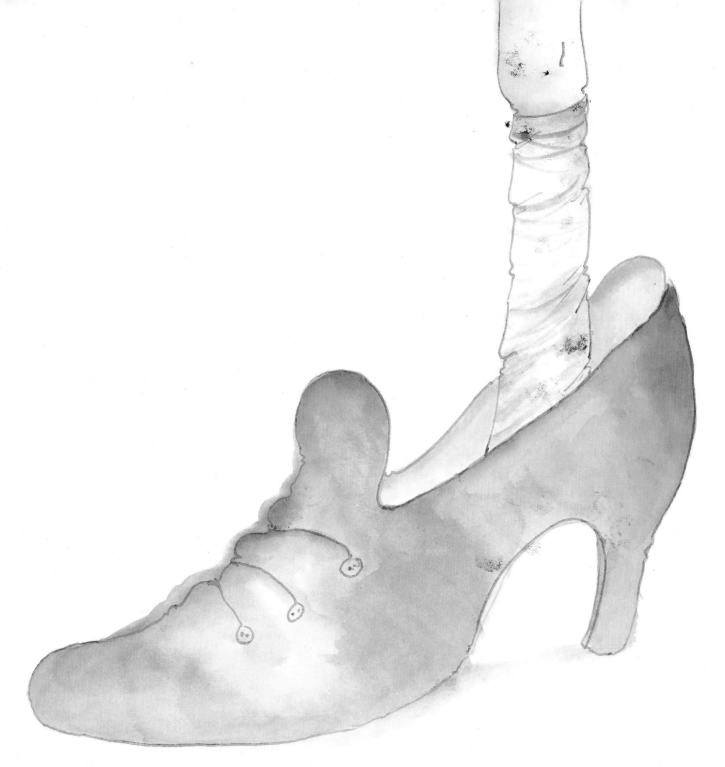

Do put the right shoes

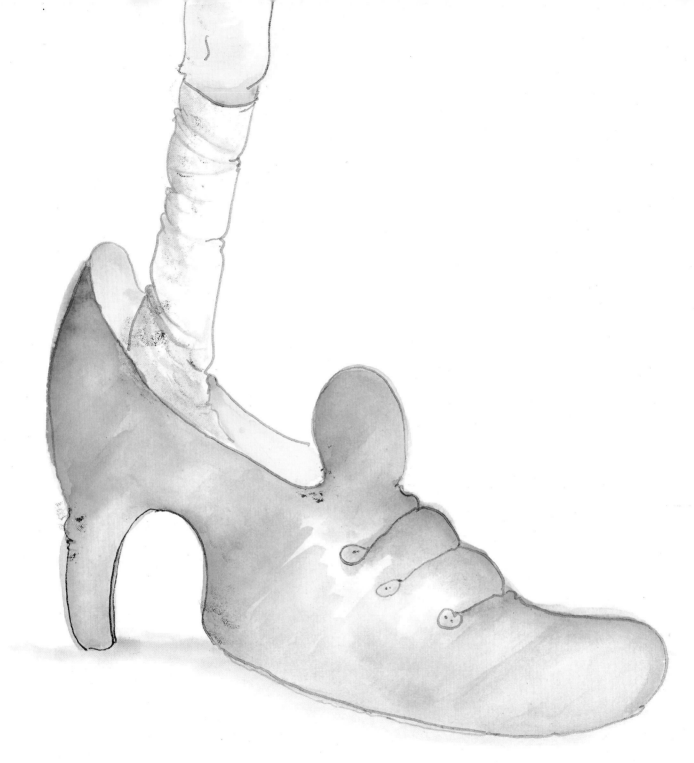

on your feet!

Do try
to mind
your own
business . . .

it's very
very rude
to peep!

Do clean up your bedroom.

Brush your hair,

brush
your teeth,

Do as you would
be done by others . . .

as much as you
possibly can!

"I really *tried!*"

First published in the United States 1996 by
Dial Books for Young Readers
A Division of Penguin Books USA Inc.
375 Hudson Street
New York, New York 10014

Published in Great Britain 1995 by Hamish Hamilton Ltd.
Copyright © 1995 by Babette Cole
All rights reserved
Printed in Italy by L.E.G.O.
First Edition
1 3 5 7 9 10 8 6 4 2

Library of Congress Cataloging in Publication Data
Cole, Babette.
The bad good manners book / Babette Cole.
p.   cm.
Summary: A lighthearted look at etiquette for the young.
ISBN 0-8037-2006-8 (hc)
1. Etiquette for children and teenagers—Juvenile literature.
[1. Etiquette.] I. Title.
BJ1857.C5C65   1996   395—dc20   95-34569   CIP   AC

The art was prepared using pencil and watercolor